TO MY FATHER (RAHIMULLAH), WHO TAUGHT ME TO BE
MYSELF FULLY, OPENLY, AND WITHOUT SHAME
–J.T.-B.

FOR THOSE WHO ARE STRUGGLING TO FIND A PLACE
–H.A.

Text copyright © 2023 by Jamilah Thompkins-Bigelow
Jacket art and interior illustrations copyright © 2023 by Hatem Aly

All rights reserved. Published in the United States by Random House Studio,
an imprint of Random House Children's Books,
a division of Penguin Random House LLC, New York.

Random House Studio with colophon is a trademark of Penguin Random House LLC.

Visit us on the Web! rhcbooks.com

Educators and librarians, for a variety of teaching tools, visit us at RHTeachersLibrarians.com

Library of Congress Cataloging-in-Publication Data is available upon request.
ISBN 978-1-9848-4809-3 (trade) — ISBN 978-1-9848-4810-9 (lib. bdg.) — ISBN 978-1-9848-4811-6 (ebook)

The artist used digital rendering in Adobe Photoshop along with scans
of ink washes and textures to create the artwork for this book.
The text of this book is set in 14-point Ionic No 5.
Interior design by Rachael Cole & Paula Baver

MANUFACTURED IN CHINA
10 9 8 7 6 5 4 3 2 1
First Edition

Random House Children's Books supports the First Amendment
and celebrates the right to read.

SALAT IN SECRET

WORDS BY
JAMILAH THOMPKINS-BIGELOW

ART BY
HATEM ALY

RANDOM HOUSE STUDIO ▲ NEW YORK

Daddy's joy is bigger than him. It's a wide, gap-toothed smile and a deep rumbling laugh that shakes the dinner table kind of joy. That joy is biggest on my birthday when he gives me a salat rug.

"You're seven now, Muhammad! Old enough to pray five times a day!"

I run my finger along the rug's fuzzy patterns and gold stitching. Its too-sweet incense smell tickles my nose.

Before prayer that night, I make wudu, washing carefully.

During salat, I don't rock and sway. My fingers don't tap-dance. No making funny faces at Maryama. I am too old for that now.

I am still. Like Daddy. When I press my forehead on that velvety rug, I repeat words learned in Sunday school. I whisper my most-wished-for wishes to Allah.

After I pray fajr the next morning, I know I'll do dhuhr too. Dhuhr comes in the middle of the school day. Somehow, I'll find a secret place to do it. Somehow, asking won't be scary.

Daddy doesn't need secret places. Whenever
I work on his ice cream truck and the sun sets,
even though we're far from a masjid, he parks
and spreads his rug on the sidewalk.

"Never delay salat," he says.

Once, some teenagers laughed. Daddy
kept moving up and down, slow and brave.

I watched from the truck, hands shaking.

When I get to school,
I see what I need: space
to bow. A door that shuts.
No windows. A room that
can keep a secret.
   Would Mrs. Baker let me
pray in the coat closet?

I don't know Mrs. Baker well. But I know she gives things—candies with riddles on the wrappers and rocket-shaped bookmarks. And smiles. She gives lots of smiles. I go to her.

"Hi, Muhammad. Do you need something?"

I open my mouth. I try to push my question out, but in my head, I see people staring at Daddy. I hear rough laughs. Would Mrs. Baker think salat is funny?

"Mrs. Baker!" Ella calls.

I rush to my desk. I'll ask when Mrs. Baker isn't busy.

Mrs. Baker reads aloud an adventure.

She referees our math relay race.

She leads a spelling bee.

She has no time for my quiet question.

By lunch, I decide to find another place.

Splashing my feet is tricky in the nurse's office bathroom.

I think about praying there, but I don't want to bow next to the toilet.

At recess, I creep behind a large oak.
"Where are you going, Muhammad?
We're playing over there!" Chris yells.

Kicking a goal while hiding a rug doesn't make me feel better.

After recess, I wait.

When everyone
leaves the closet,
I throw my rug down.

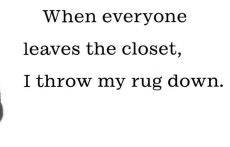

I begin.

Sunday school
words sprint from
my lips. No wishes.
Not enough time.

"Quiet, please!" Mrs. Baker
yells from the classroom.
"Get settled!"

"Take out your notebooks,"
Mrs. Baker says.

I fling myself into a bow.

I swing back up.

Then, "Where is
Muhammad?"

"Can I check?"
I hear Chris ask.

The Sunday school words trip and stumble over each other. I drop to the floor, up, down, up, quick! I stand to do it again. When I hear footsteps, I snatch up the rug.

"What's taking you so long? What's that?" Chris asks.

"Nothing," I grumble.

I don't pray until I get home. I wish for bravery.

After salat, Daddy asks me to go out with him. The cool air is nagging Daddy to park his ice cream truck for the year.

But for one more week, we can be ice cream men together.

On the truck, I make my joy big and my
face sunny like Daddy does for customers.

I feel that sunniness inside too.

But soon the sun sets.

Daddy takes out his rug. "You can always pray when you get home."

I don't say that I brought my rug too.

Daddy spreads his rug outside.

A woman walks past, then stops. She can't
see Daddy is an ice cream man with joy bigger
than him. Daddy is just big and strange.

Some officers try talking.
Daddy prays.

My rug shakes in
my hand. I pull the
door handle.

"We're just ice cream men praying."
I push the quivery words out. I spread my
rug beside Daddy's.

I see his hands tremble. His words quiver
like mine. We pray, slow and brave and
shaky. The officers watch. Then they leave.

I stand at Mrs. Baker's desk the next day.

"Mrs. Baker, I'm a Muslim, and I need somewhere to pray." My voice shakes, but I now know bravery sometimes comes with shaking.

COATS

She smiles. "Of course, Muhammad.
Let's find you a place."

"I know a good one," I say.

AUTHOR'S NOTE

Salat (suh-LOT) is a structured form of prayer that observant Muslims perform five times a day. While Muslims worship in multiple ways, salat is considered a pillar of the Islamic faith. Each salat takes place during a fixed span of time:

Fajr (FAH-jir): dawn to sunrise
Dhuhr (DH-oo-r): midday
Asr (OSS-ir): afternoon
Maghrib (muh-GHREB): sunset to night
Isha (ee-SHAA): night

Muslim children practice salat from a young age. In fact, many begin as toddlers. Age seven is when children are instructed to observe all five prayers. Salat consists of a set series of movements: standing, bowing, standing, prostrating, sitting, prostrating, then sitting up again. While in these positions, people recite verses from the Quran and other Islamic texts. They may also make dua, or ask Allah to fulfill a wish. The series is repeated two to four times in the daily prayers.

OTHER TERMS

Allah (uhl-LAW): Arabic word for God.

Dua (doo-AH): A prayer that makes a request. Dua can be made at any time, including during salat.

Masjid (MAS-jid): Islamic place of worship. This is the Arabic word that "mosque" comes from.

Muslim (MUSS-lim): A person whose religion is Islam. There are almost two billion Muslims in the world.

Quran (coor-AHN): The religious text of Islam. Muslims memorize verses of the Quran and recite them in prayer.

Salat (suh-LOT) rug: Many Muslims use a rug to create a clean barrier between their bodies and the ground when they perform salat. Other common names include "sajadah" and "janamaz."

Wudu (WOOD-oo): A quick cleansing that Muslims do before prayer. They wash their hands, mouth, nose, face, arms, head, ears, and feet with water.

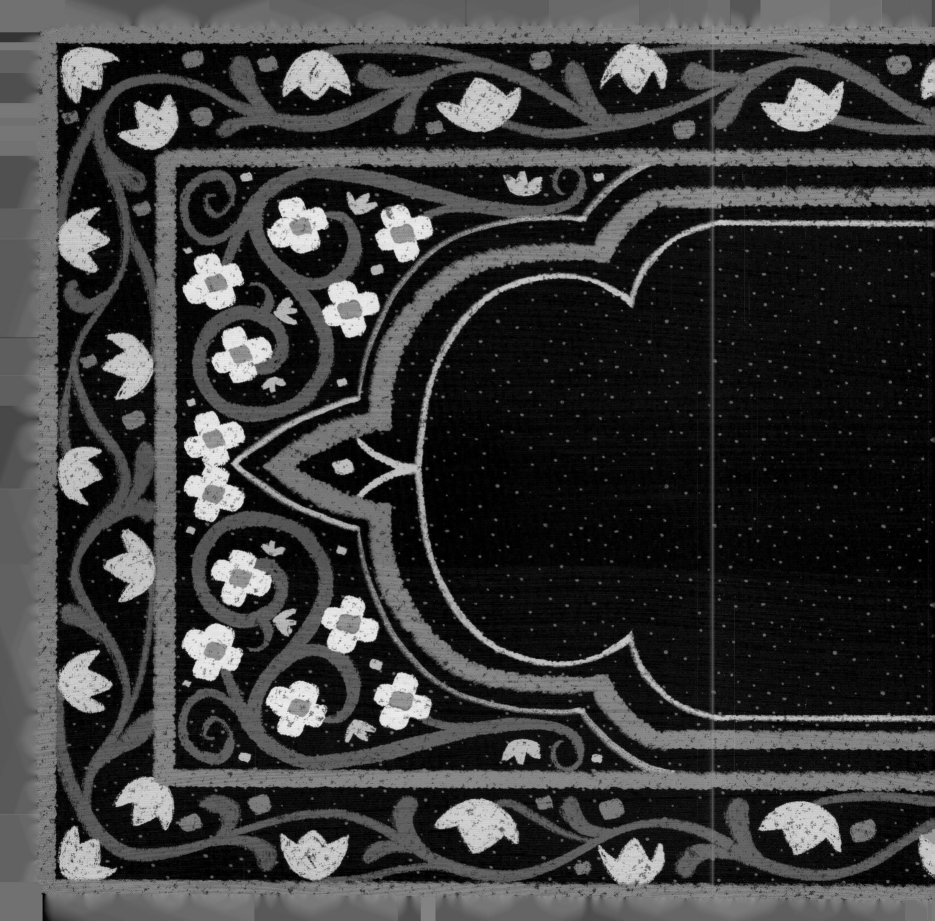